SPACE

Exploring the Moon, the Planets,
and Beyond

Library of Congress Cataloging-in-Publication Data has been applied for.
ISBN: 0-8109-5719-1

Copyright © 2006 Éditions de La Martinière, Paris
English translation copyright © 2006 Abrams Books for Young Readers, New York

Published in 2006 by Abrams Books for Young Readers, an imprint of Harry N. Abrams, Inc.

Printed and bound in Belgium
10 9 8 7 6 5 4 3 2 1

HNA
harry n. abrams, inc.
a subsidiary of La Martinière Groupe
115 West 18th Street
New York, NY 10011
www.hnabooks.com

SPACE

Exploring the Moon, the Planets, and Beyond

Text by
Olivier de Goursac

Illustrations by
Pascal Laye

ABRAMS BOOKS FOR YOUNG READERS
NEW YORK

CONTENTS

Introduction 10

3, 2, 1… Lift-off!

Space: A Vast Emptiness Waiting to Be Explored 12

Early Dreams of Space Travel .14

Making a Rocket Is So Easy 16

Getting into Space Is More Complicated 18

A Rocket + an Aircraft = the Space Shuttle 20

Living in Space .22

What Use Is space?

Space and the Military 24

Satellites: The Advantages of Robots in Orbit 26

The Need for a Human Presence 28

Into Orbit!

Animals: Pioneers in Space 30

A Wonderful Human Adventure 32

Living in Space .34

Walking in Space 36

The Space Station: A World in Miniature 38

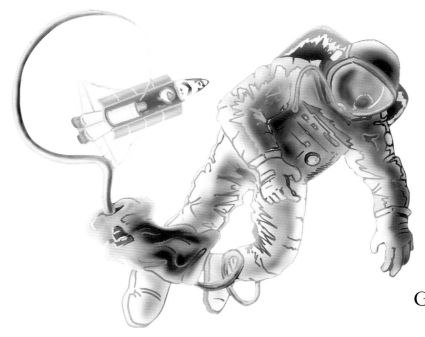

Destination Moon

Getting to the Moon 40

Landing on the Moon 42

Walking on the Moon 44

Getting Around on the Moon 46

Reaching for Other Worlds

Venus: A Living Hell 48

Mars: A Difficult Place to Land 50

Mars: Meticulously Mapped 52

Asteroids: Flying Mountains 54

Penetrating Jupiter 56

Titan: Fog, Wind, and Ice 58

Uranus: Near the Rings 60

Neptune: A Cold, Dark Giant 62

Pluto: Surviving Away from the Sun 64

Space, a New Continent

Living on the Moon 66

A City in Space 68

The First People on Mars 70

Building a Base on Mars 72

Traveling to Another Star 74

Introduction . . .

In 1970, I was your age and men had just walked on the Moon for the first time.

With my construction kits, I used to make lunar modules with feet mounted on springs and drop them from the top of the stairs on a piece of string to see if they would touch down safely . . . I would build space stations, hang them from the ceiling, and man them with little turtles, which moved from module to module in search of their food . . . turtles in space!

In the 1960s and 1970s, space travel was a great adventure which inspired children . . . and their parents!

Today, though not everyone can be an astronaut, space is part of our daily lives, thanks to films like *Star Wars*, *Starship Troopers*, and *Mission to Mars*. But the picture these movies paint is far from reality.

For example, in space a spaceship does not make a noise, as there is no air to carry the sound. Nor does it fly or turn like an airplane. It does not need to have its engines working all the time. To travel, it fires them up for just a few minutes, then shuts them down again. The spaceship can then continue on its course in a straight line, as there is no air to slow it down.

Despite what you see in films, space is a hostile and dangerous environment. You cannot go outside your spacecraft without a spacesuit to protect you from the surrounding vacuum and extreme temperatures. In sunlight, the temperature is 480° F (250° C), in the shade it's minus 420°F (minus 250°C)! If you make even the slightest mistake, you're done for!

But space exploration is well worth it. The useful technical discoveries that have been made are endless. You can already see the evidence in your own home. In seeking to protect equipment from heat, scientists invented the Teflon now used in frying pans. To enable astronauts to attach anything anywhere, scientists invented Velcro strips. To calculate the trajectories of rockets more quickly, they developed the processors now used in personal computers . . .

Space spells adventure, real adventure, with all its dangers and possibilities for discovery. You belong to a generation which may be fortunate enough to take off into space, just as people fly by airplane today. You will see men and women travel to the Moon, land on Mars, and maybe journey even further . . .

This is your universe.
Let's take off into space!

— Olivier de Goursac

Space: A Vast Emptiness Waiting to Be Explored

Space is far from empty. Here you can see a vast cloud of gas in the Eagle Nebula. At its center some young blue stars have just been born. The heat they emit drives the gas away.

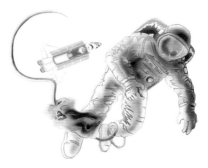

What is "space"? In theory, it is the void separating everything that fills the universe: the planets and their moons (the small satellites that revolve around them), the stars, and even galaxies. In fact, space is not empty at all. The space between the Earth and the Moon, for example, is full of tiny molecules (combinations of even smaller particles we call atoms). It contains between one thousand and one million atoms per cubic inch—though this is a very small number compared to the multitude of atoms circulating inside Earth's atmosphere. Between the stars, too, there are thin clouds of gases (hydrogen and helium) which carry a fine dust consisting of carbon, silicon (minerals from which rocks are formed), and ice.

People have always wanted to break free of the Earth and explore this emptiness, and this has led to the "conquest" of space. Space travel was conceived of by far-sighted engineers who have looked for, and found, technical solutions to make it possible for humans to enter space. And when human beings are unable to go to certain places, because they are too remote or too dangerous, they have sent robots instead. What a great adventure space can be!

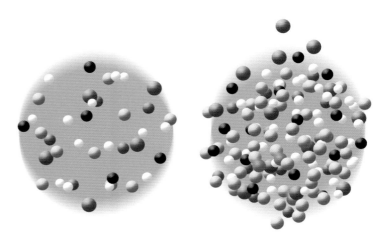

Matter consists of atoms. They are far more numerous in the Earth's atmosphere (pictured on the right) than in the void of space (pictured at left).

Early Dreams of Space Travel

Jules Verne's intrepid space travelers watch as their spaceship hurtles toward the Moon; a phenomenon experienced by astronauts today. On the right, a "space train," imagined by Jules Verne as a way of sending people to the Moon.

People have always looked at the sky and dreamed. In the seventeenth century, writers were already telling stories of travelers who had been to the Moon. These were fantastic tales in which people visited space in balloons or by climbing a moonbeam. Hardly based in reality!

In the nineteenth century, people began thinking seriously of going into space. The literature of the time reflected scientific research and knowledge. Jules Verne's two novels *From the Earth to the Moon* and *Round the Moon* (1865 and 1870), described space travel more realistically, with astronauts "floating" because of weightlessness. These stories were to influence the scientific research of the fathers of space travel: the Russian Konstantin Tsiolkovsky (1857–1935) and the Hungarian Hermann Oberth (1894–1989), who first had the idea of building a rocket engine. They considered all aspects of how rockets might fly: the paths they would need to take through space, and ways of getting a rocket to orbit around the Earth.

The first science-fiction novels also made people dream. After the publication of H.G. Wells's *War of the Worlds* (1898), many people thought that Mars was inhabited and longed to go and explore it! But it was not until the twentieth century that these dreams began to come true. Between 1926 and 1945, the great pioneers of space exploration—the American Robert Goddard, the Russian Sergei Korolev, and the German Wernher von Braun—built and launched the first rockets.

Jules Verne imagined sending men to the Moon in a capsule fired like a shell from a huge cannon!

Making a Rocket Is Easy

Supervised by adults, some young people launch a model rocket, at left. They stand at a safe distance to avoid being burned by the flames as their rocket takes off. On the right, the fuse of a firework rocket is lit.

It is easy to launch an object into the air using another object—propelling an arrow with a bow, for example. But a rocket has to lift off the ground by itself, so it must have an engine. It is possible to make a "water rocket" with a plastic bottle, with the bottle itself acting as the engine. You fill the bottle halfway with water, then compress the air it contains and close it with a stopper. As soon as the stopper is released, the compressed air pushes against the water and the bottle jumps into the air. This is the "action-reaction" principle at work: A strong downward thrust produces an opposite upward movement. A water rocket is the easiest kind of rocket to make.

Model rockets are powered by gunpowder, a tightly compressed chemical propellant as hard as stone. When you light a match below the chemical engine it catches fire very quickly and produces a gas so hot and powerful that it pushes the rocket upward.

For maximum speed, a rocket must be able to cut through the surrounding air as smoothly as possible. This is why rockets are long and slender, and end in a pointed cone, whether they are mere model rockets or really large space rockets.

The purpose of a rocket is to send objects (or people) into the air or into space. The object a rocket carries is called the "payload." The payload may be a colorful firework; in the case of a large launcher rocket, a satellite (an object designed to circle the Earth); or even a space capsule (a cabin to transport humans into space). The payload is always put inside the "nose" of the rocket.

When the king of France received visitors at Versailles, rockets were used to launch fireworks into the air. Let the fun begin!

Getting into Space Is More Complicated

On the left, the two engines of a *Titan* rocket. In the center, lift-off of the giant *Saturn 5* rocket. When it reaches an altitude of about 30 miles (50 kilometers), its first section is discarded (right) as the second section takes over and continues to power it into space.

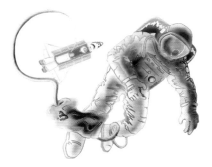

To launch a satellite into orbit around the Earth (in other words, to get it to circle the Earth), you have to overcome the Earth's power of attraction, known as "gravity." The faster a rocket travels, the more easily it can overcome this force. A speed of 17,670 miles per hour (28,440 kilometers per hour) is ideal for countering the force which pulls an object back toward the Earth. If launched at this speed, a satellite will not fall back to Earth, nor will it completely break away from the Earth's gravitational field. Instead, it very quickly begins to travel in circles around the Earth.

If a satellite travels at less than 4.9 miles per second (7.9 kilometers per second), the power of the Earth's gravity will pull it back down. If, on the other hand, it goes any faster, the satellite will not go into orbit but will travel out into space. Fortunately, engineers have found ways of making rockets smaller so that they use less fuel. Fuel is heavy to carry and the whole purpose of a rocket is to carry a payload into space, not fuel tanks! To make rockets lighter as they climb into space, they are designed to shed their fuel tanks once the fuel in them is used up. Rockets are therefore divided into a number of sections (or "stages"), each with its own fuel tanks and engine. When the fuel tanks of one section are empty, they are discarded and the rocket becomes that much lighter. The following section then begins to propel the rocket. And all this happens very quickly. Once a rocket has been launched, it takes on average just ten minutes to go into orbit!

1—Spacecraft (capsule) to go into orbit
2—Third section
3—Second section discarded shortly before the spacecraft is launched into orbit
4—First section discarded at an altitude of 30 miles (50 kilometers)

A Rocket + an Aircraft = the Space Shuttle

The shuttle takes off: The spacecraft is attached to the large, brown-colored central fuel tank. In the foreground, you can see one of the solid-fuel rockets that will propel it into space.

Forty years ago, engineers thought of a less expensive way of getting into space: the space shuttle, a reusable vehicle that did not need to shed its fuel tanks when the fuel was used up. Originally, it consisted of a small aircraft, fixed to a much larger one which served as the rocket for launching the shuttle. The larger aircraft separated from the shuttle when it reached the right height, leaving the shuttle to continue its journey into orbit. Inside the payload bay of the shuttle was mounted a cylindrical cabin (the space module)—a little apartment in which seven astronauts could live and work for at least two weeks. After each flight, the shuttle returned to earth and landed, like an airplane. In 1972, because money was short, NASA (the National Aeronautics and Space Administration) decided to replace the large launcher aircraft with two long rocket engines placed on either side of a large central fuel tank. This system, while less expensive, was no longer entirely reusable, because the fuel tank and propulsion units had to be discarded after take-off.

The space shuttle did have other disadvantages. The "half aircraft, half rocket" concept was dangerous during take-off, because the shuttle had been designed to leave the ground horizontally, like an airplane, and it was being made to take off vertically, like a rocket. Of the five shuttles built, two have had disastrous accidents, killing their crews (one during take-off and one during landing). Only three shuttles now remain in service.

Living in Space

The large International Space Station (ISS), visited each year by dozens of astronauts of different nationalities, orbits the Earth. Large solar panels deployed on either side generate its electricity supply.

Astronauts have to be able to stay up in space for long periods of time, but there is often not enough room on board a space module to store all the things they need for a long journey (air, water, food, and so on).

One solution is to build a base (or "station") for them up in space. The idea is to assemble a number of space modules, in which astronauts can live and work in more comfortable conditions for longer periods of time. The first such bases were the American Skylab space station (1973–1974), and the Russian Saliout and Mir stations (1970–2001). Then the Americans, Russians, Japanese, and Europeans decided to build the large International Space Station (ISS), which is still under construction today. This can accommodate up to ten astronauts, some of whom remain in space for more than six months!

In the ISS, electricity is produced from the sun's rays using solar panels. The astronauts' time is divided between maintenance tasks, scientific experiments, and keeping fit. Because they "float" in a weightless environment, the astronauts do not need to make any effort to stand upright or move around to get things, and their muscles would waste (or "atrophy") if they did not follow a daily exercise regime. These space travelers also have some leisure time, which they generally spend viewing and taking photographs of the Earth.

An automated arm takes hold of a module to moor it to the space station.

Space and the Military

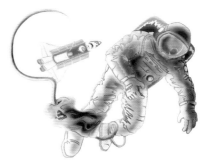

On the left, a rocket launching the *Soyuz* capsule into space (the small photograph shows the R7 missile that inspired this rocket). On the right, a *Titan* rocket launches the *Gemini* capsule (the small photograph shows the same type of rocket, but designed for military use).

Going farther and faster in space is a foremost concern of the armed forces. They often have the largest budgets for inventing new weapons and building more efficient machines. Their aim is to always stay ahead of potential enemies.

But technical and scientific discoveries made for national defense may also be used for non-military purposes. After a certain time, the veil of secrecy is lifted because newer and better technologies have replaced older ones. These inventions can then be applied in daily life. One example of this is Teflon: Now used in frying pans, this material was first invented for military purposes.

The same is true of inventions made in name of space exploration. The biggest technical advances were made after 1945, when Americans and Russians were competing to build rockets capable of sending nuclear warheads to other continents. These rockets were so powerful that they could also be used for launching satellites or sending astronauts up in space capsules to orbit the Earth. And so civilian versions came to be built. The armed forces now use satellites for spying on other countries, forecasting the weather in preparation for military campaigns, and keeping in touch with soldiers on the battlefield. Some day these same satellites may be used for more everyday purposes.

On a battlefield, soldiers fire missiles at the enemy.

Satellites: The Advantages of Robots in Orbit

On the left, men in sterile clothing make final adjustments to a satellite before it is launched into orbit. On the right, a view of the Mississippi River delta on Earth, taken from a satellite.

In space, machines are often more efficient than human beings, especially for performing repetitive tasks. When it comes to observing the Earth or transmitting messages from one part of the globe to another, a robot can be very effective. Also, sending people into space is expensive, because you need to build a space capsule for them to live and work in, and to protect them from the surrounding vacuum. This is why computer-run satellites are now used for a number of specialized functions.

Satellites generate their own energy using solar panels, and so do not need to be supplied with electricity from Earth. They have small engines to ensure they are always facing in the right direction.

Today there are two main types of satellites. First, satellites that circle the Earth in a few hours at an altitude of between 155 and 250 miles (250 and 400 kilometers) above the planet's surface. These are used for taking detailed pictures and, using a global positioning system (GPS), can tell us exactly where we are. Others orbit at an altitude of 322,400 miles (6,000 kilometers). They are so distant from the Earth that it takes them up to a day to complete their orbits. Since they are so far away, it would be impossible to go and repair them. When they break down, the technicians who control them from Earth simply fire up their engines and send them deeper into space, and other satellites take their place. These far-off satellites are used for weather forecasting, telecommunications, and transmitting television broadcasts.

Building a satellite demands great precision and care to avoid potential dangers. This man is wearing a sterile suit as he makes adjustments.

The Need for a Human Presence

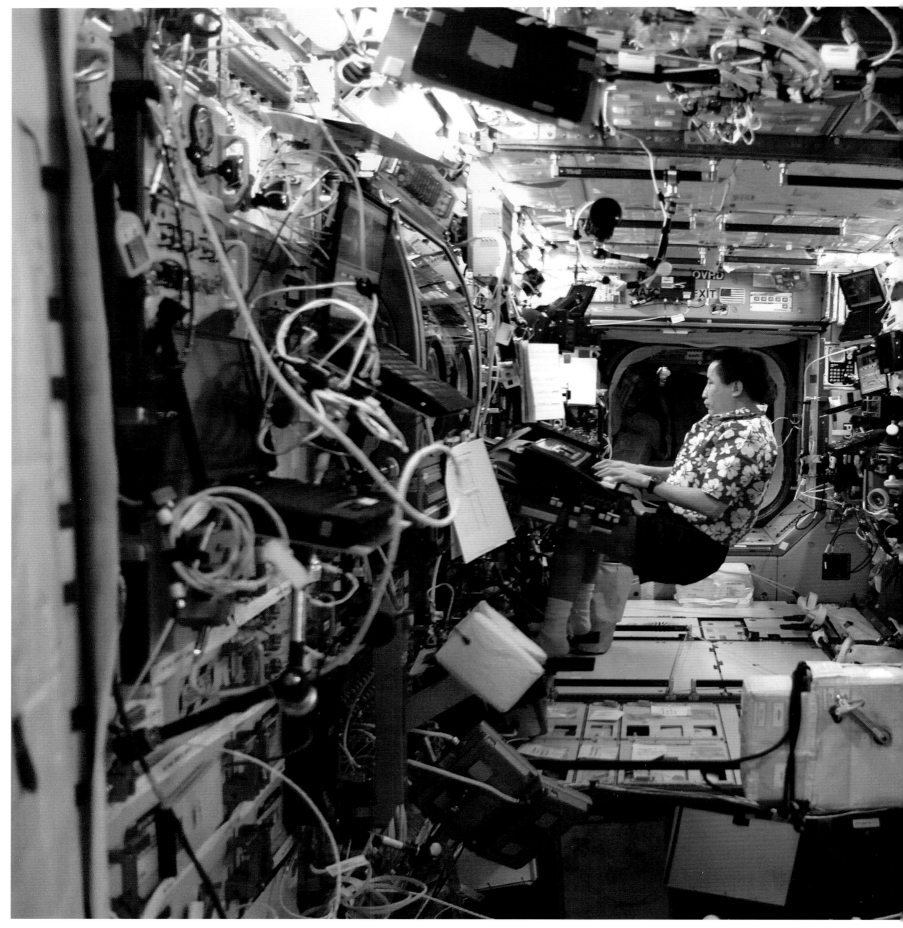

An astronaut working on one of the modules of the International Space Station. When you are weightless, you do not need a chair to sit on! The walls of the station are covered with scientific instruments.

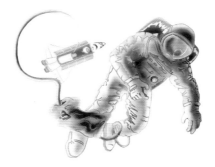

There are some things that automated machines cannot be used for in space, for example, testing materials, assembling structures, or manufacturing chemical compounds. Only human beings are capable of putting together the various modules of a space station and maneuvering them in dangerous situations. Similarly, in the event of a breakdown, a robot is not able to repair itself! For all tasks that involve making spur-of-the-moment decisions, a human presence is essential.

Moreover, in space each astronaut follows a very detailed timetable involving a large number of different duties. Imagine how many robots would be needed to replace just one human being!

For the time being, astronauts do not generally venture very far from the Earth. But the space flights they have made are enabling us to test equipment which will later be used to send people back to the Moon or to Mars. These flights also provide opportunities to measure astronauts' endurance, and see how people would cope with living in space for long periods of time.

An astronaut repairs a module using an electric screwdriver.

Animals: Pioneers in Space

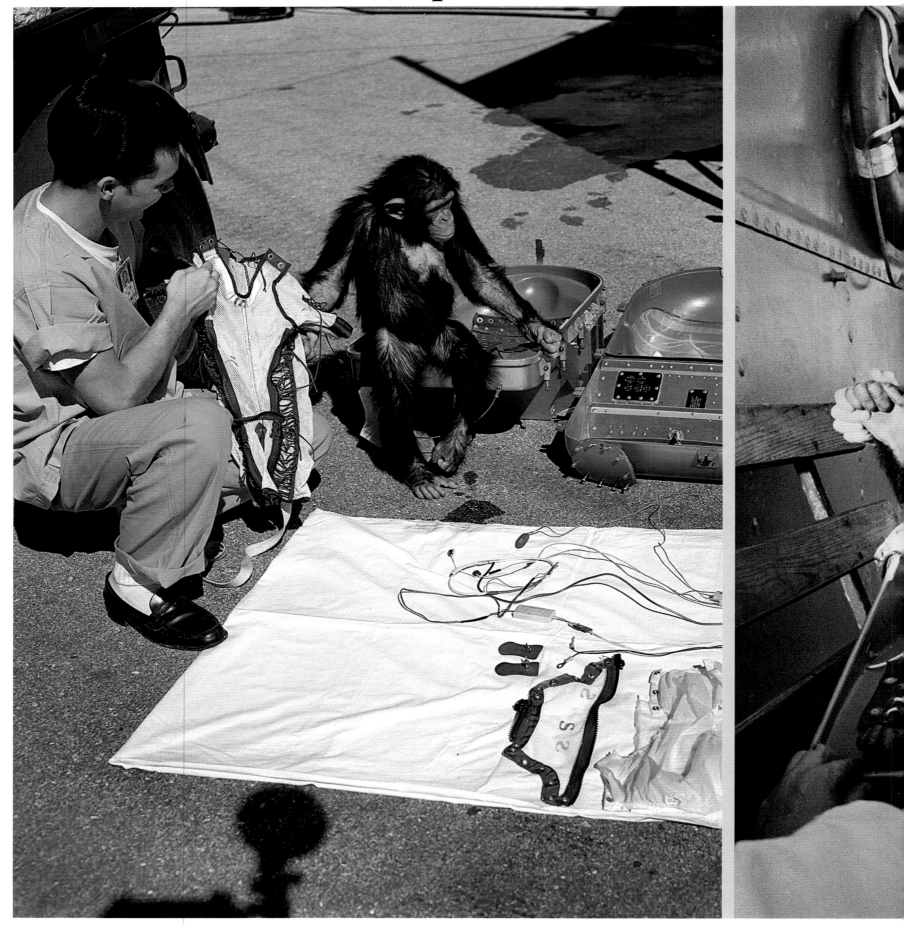

On the left, Ham, the first chimpanzee to go into space, prepares for blast-off. On the right, he shakes his commanding officer's hand after a successful landing in his *Mercury 2* space capsule.

Believe it or not, the first astronauts were animals. In 1957 a dog named Laïka traveled aboard the Russian capsule *Sputnik 2*, and in 1961 a chimpanzee called Ham went into space in the American capsule *Mercury 2*. The purpose of their journeys was to test the behavior of living beings in orbit and to find out whether exposure to solar radiation would be dangerous for humans. On Earth, we are protected from radiation by the atmosphere, but in space there is no such protective shield. The space capsule itself has to protect its occupants.

In the early days of space exploration, a number of animals unfortunately lost their lives. Nowadays, everything possible is done to ensure they return in good health. For the past 50 years, animals sent into space have included dogs, monkeys, frogs, mice, rats, a cat, flies, bees, tortoises, fish, crickets, earthworms, ants, salamanders, sea urchins, and snails.

Some animals have also been used for scientific experiments. For example, spiders and silk worms were transported into space to find out if they could adapt to weightlessness. Would they be able to weave their webs and cocoons? After a few false starts, the spider Arabella eventually spun a fine web!

Lift-off of the rocket carrying Ham into space.

A Wonderful Human Adventure

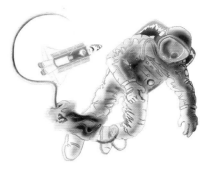

An astronaut, wearing his space suit and helmet, getting ready to go on a space walk. His companions accompany him to the exit hatch. In space, where everything floats, you can move around upside down!

In space, humans experience a state of "weightlessness." When an astronaut is in orbit, the force of gravity, which pulls him toward the Earth, is cancelled out by the speed of the spacecraft, which draws him upward. The consequences are quite amusing: Liquids, for example, freed from the effects of gravity, shape themselves into balls, as Captain Haddock and Tintin found to humorous results in the comic adventure *Explorers on the Moon*.

As he "floats" in his cabin, the astronaut may suffer from "space sickness": he loses his sense of direction and becomes queasy. Everything is therefore designed to make him feel more at ease. When he sleeps, his sleeping bag is held down with straps to give him the impression of being in a bed. In everything he does, he must be very careful: Weightless objects move very fast. If he is careless, they may collide with the walls of the capsule or the astronauts themselves.

And there is another far more serious danger. Beyond the walls of the spacecraft is the vast emptiness of space, containing no air for the astronaut to breathe. In 1997, a spacecraft bumped into a space station so violently that the wall of one of the modules was pierced and air began to escape. The astronauts had only a few minutes in which to shut the damaged module off from the rest of the station.

An astronaut sleeping. His arms rise into the air by themselves if he does not put them inside his sleeping bag.

Living in Space

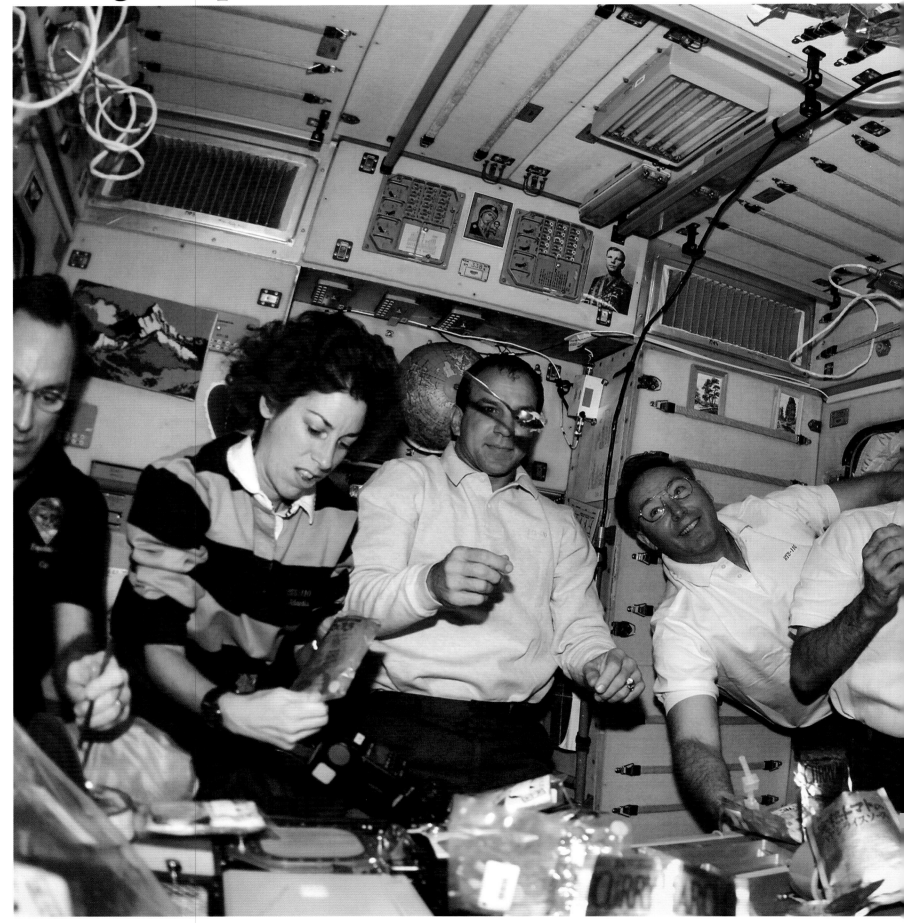

The astronauts gather together to eat. One of them has fun making his spoon float. If he wanted, he could catch it in his mouth, without using his hands!

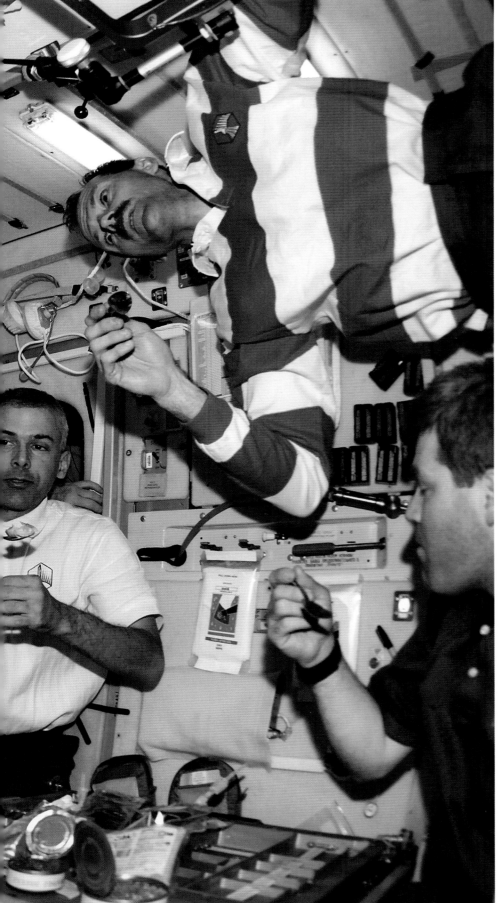

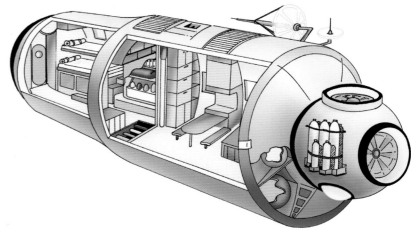

Weightlessness affects even the astronauts' most basic tasks. They therefore have to form new habits. Eating, for example, is far more difficult than on Earth, because normal kinds of food would just float around. In 1965 John Young took a large meat sandwich with him into space in his *Gemini* capsule. This infuriated mission control at NASA because the crumbs flew all over the cabin, threatening to get into the electric circuits.

These days astronauts eat frozen and dried foods (hot water has to be added to make them easier to eat). The food is put on a tray in a sticky sauce that keeps it anchored. Liquids are contained in cartons, with straws to drink them through. The real luxury on board is in fact water, as every drop has to be brought from Earth, and it takes up a lot of space. The rules for washing are therefore very strict. Astronauts may take showers, but there is a system that immediately sucks up the waste water. Otherwise, it would fly around and cause short-circuits. The toilets work in the same way: everything is immediately vacuumed up. A purification plant then recycles the liquids. The same water is used for washing or drinking over and over again.

Living accommodations in a space station.

Walking in Space

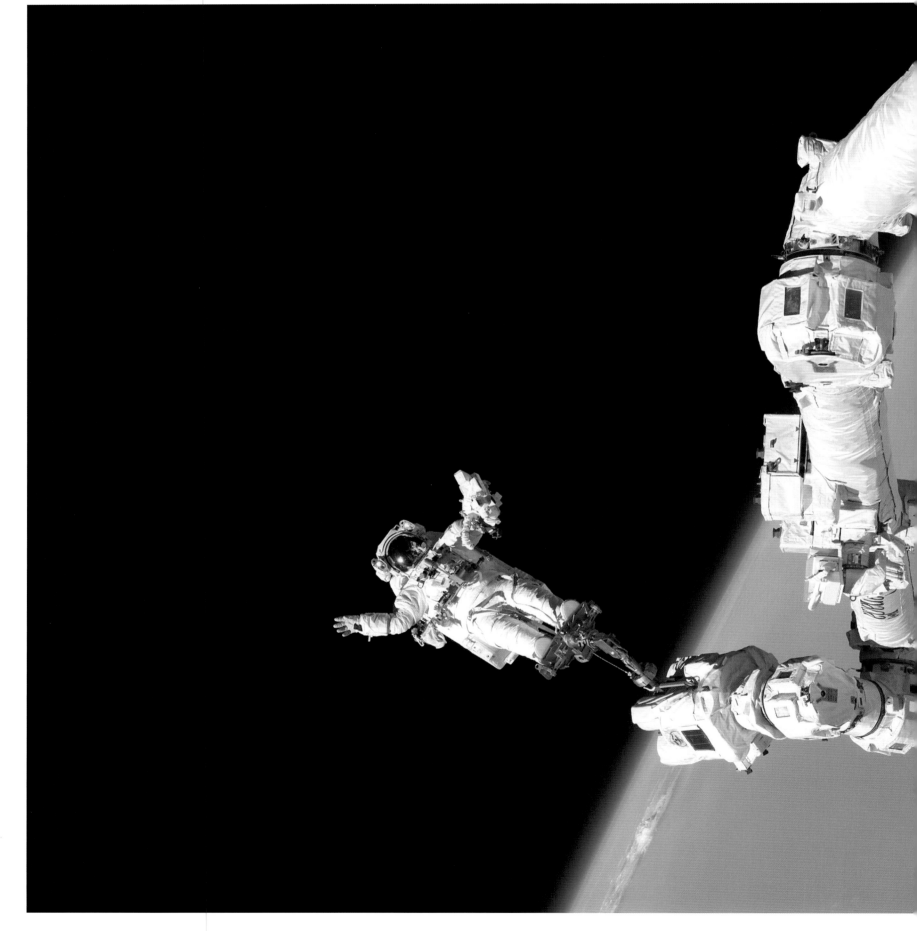

Attached to the shuttle's mechanical arm, an astronaut gets ready to repair the ship. He waves his hand at the rest of the crew, who have remained onboard. He has a superb view of the Earth from this position.

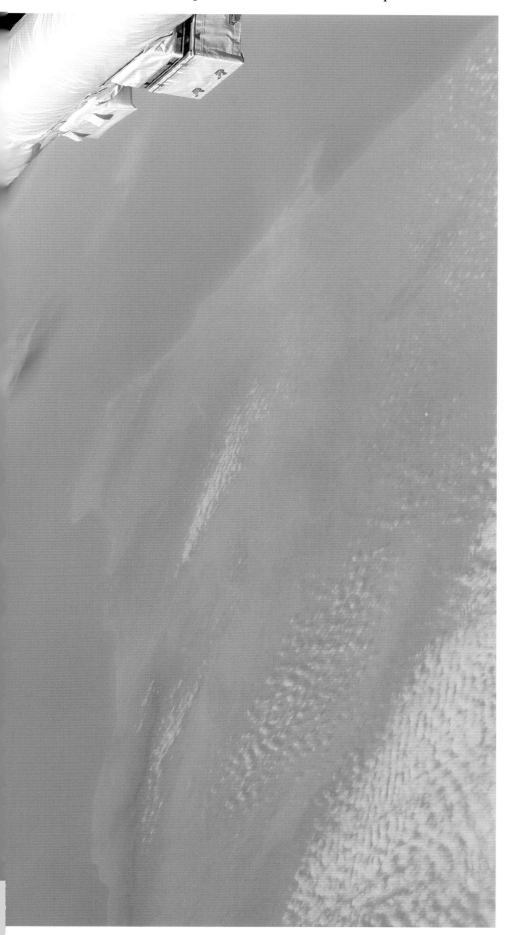

When an astronaut leaves the spacecraft, he is said to be performing an Extra-Vehicular Activity (EVA). He must wear a space suit to protect him from the vacuum outside and enable him to breathe, and carry his air reserves in his backpack. If he is thirsty, he can drink with his helmet on, sucking water through a straw from another part of his backpack. An EVA may last up to eight hours.

When an astronaut has to work for many hours in the same position, to repair a satellite for example, he stands at the end of a long articulated arm attached to the spacecraft, his feet fixed to a small platform. The tools he uses have broad handles, specially designed for the thick fingers of his gloves.

Space-walking can be dangerous. When you are in a state of weightlessness, the smallest mistake can be fatal. If pieces of equipment, like the large modules of the space station, are not guided accurately, they may crush the astronaut, or crash into the station and cause serious damage. To avoid drifting off into space, the astronaut must always remember to attach his space suit to the articulated arm, except on missions when he has to go some distance from the spacecraft, for example to secure a satellite. The astronaut then sits at the controls of a Manned Maneuvering Unit (MMU), a kind of "space armchair," which he steers by firing small rocket engines.

There is nothing like an MMU (Manned Maneuvering Unit) for getting around in space!

The Space Station: A World in Miniature

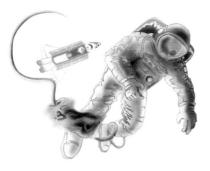

An astronaut takes photographs of the Earth as it rotates beneath him. The beauty of our planet is truly amazing.

Despite their busy schedules, astronauts on a space station are allowed rest breaks from time to time. They may take personal items onboard to make themselves feel at home. They play cards, read, listen to CDs, and even make music. Sometimes, as a special treat, they are sent fresh fruit from Earth.

Astronauts spending time on a space station must be able to speak several languages, as there are often representatives of several countries on the station—Americans, Russians, Europeans, Asians—reflecting the Earth's diversity in space.

Astronauts often use their leisure time to observe and photograph the Earth. Seen from space, it is incredibly beautiful. Landscapes pass before their eyes at great speed, as they circle the Earth in 90 minutes. Frontiers and individual countries do not exist. So when they return to Earth, astronauts often have a very different view of our world. They all say that, seen from space, the Earth looks fragile and in need of protection. On returning from the Moon, some have also described how very small they felt, seeing the Earth as a tiny blue ball floating in the immensity of the cosmos.

To prevent their muscles from losing strength, the astronauts work out on exercise machines every day.

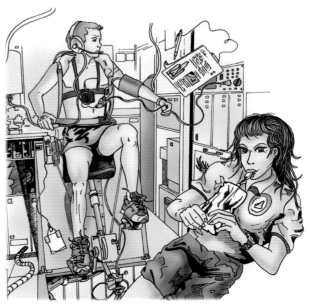

Getting to the Moon

The heroes who have just walked on the Moon are back aboard the lunar module, ready to return to the *Apollo* capsule, which has remained in orbit. In the background, there is a magnificent "earthrise."

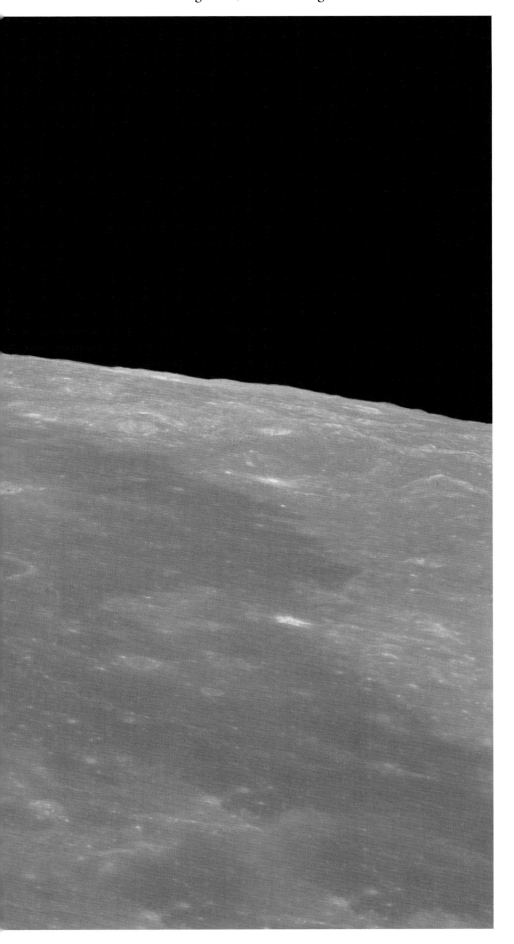

Going to the Moon might not seem like such an amazing achievement today, but for thousands of years it seemed an impossible dream . . . until one fine day in 1969. The story began after the Second World War. A new generation of engineers had been born and all kinds of dreams were becoming possible.

At that time, the United States and Russia were engaged in furious competition. Both wanted to take the lead in weapons research, science, and technology. This is why space exploration developed so quickly. In 1962, President Kennedy promised his fellow countrymen that by 1970 two Americans would go to the Moon and come back to Earth safe and sound—a daring adventure to show the world the superiority of American technology. A gigantic scientific and industrial effort got under way. NASA launched the Apollo program, which resulted in the construction of a series of enormous rockets—the biggest, *Saturn 5*, was 360 feet (110 meters) tall—and the *Apollo* space capsule, capable of carrying three astronauts to the Moon. Another essential part of the plan was the lunar module (LM), designed to enable two men to land safely on the Moon, then rejoin the third crew member orbiting the Moon in *Apollo*, before heading back to Earth. President Kennedy's bold declaration triggered an amazing and inspiring human adventure, full of excitement and with important consequences.

The path of the *Apollo* spacecraft formed a large figure eight between the Earth and the Moon.

Landing on the Moon

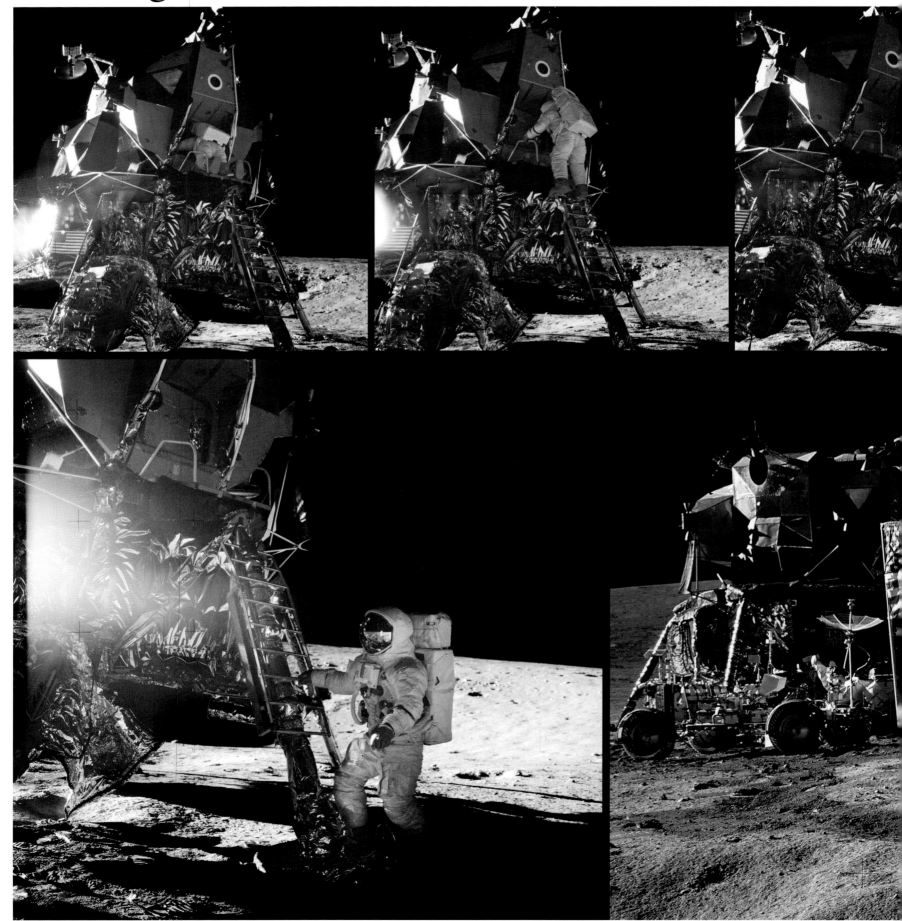

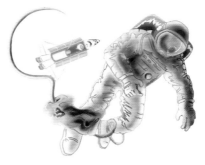

An astronaut descends the lunar module's ladder to walk on the Moon. In the bottom right, John Young sends a greeting to earth by jumping three feet high. Here he is only one sixth of his normal weight.

NASA first tested the *Apollo* spacecraft in orbit around the Earth. Then they decided to send it on eight missions to the Moon. The astronauts lived in the *Apollo* capsule. Attached to it was another module, which supplied it with electricity, air, and water. The third component was the lunar module (LM), a small spacecraft designed for landing astronauts on the Moon. Together, these modules formed a small apartment in which the astronauts could move around during the three days it took to reach the Moon.

Once they were in orbit around the Moon, two astronauts took their places in the LM and separated from the *Apollo* capsule. It took them three hours to reach the Moon's surface and during the landing they controlled the LM manually. It was a risky business, as they had only enough fuel to make one attempt. After a rest period, they put on their space suits and the big survival packs containing their air and water supplies, and opened the exit hatch. Carefully, they descended the ladder, and at last they were walking on the Moon! Their first task was to load some pieces of rock onto the LM, so that scientists would know what the Moon is made of. They then went back onboard the module and closed the hatch. One astronaut set up a hammock to sleep in, while the other slept on the floor. Further expeditions were planned for the second and third days. When the mission was completed, the spacecraft took off from the Moon's surface, but only the upper part of the LM rejoined the orbiting *Apollo* capsule; the rest was left behind.

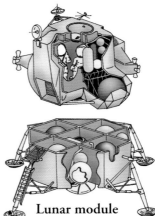

Lunar module (LM)

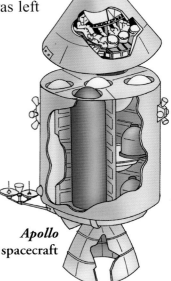

Apollo spacecraft

Walking on the Moon

An astronaut walking beside one of the Moon's craters. Note that the Moon's surface is a uniform gray.

When walking on the Moon, you have to be careful not to get carried away, as you weigh only one sixth of your normal weight. It is much easier to slip and fall over. The astronauts soon developed a rolling gait, moving sideways from one foot to the other, to slow themselves down.

The astronauts had many adventures while on the Moon. Some got lost, unable to read their maps and identify the landmarks around them. Another thought he had found a strange stone and put it in his bag, but it turned out to be a piece of polystyrene packing material covered in lunar dust! They also took shots with two golf balls, making a club from the handles of the shovels they used for taking samples. And one managed to repair the broken mudguard of his lunar "jeep" by stapling maps together.

Astronauts also investigated an old space probe that had landed on the Moon two years earlier, cutting pieces off to take back to Earth. It was discovered that microbes from Earth had managed to survive, though they should have died in the vacuum of space. Conclusion: Microbes are far more resilient than human beings!

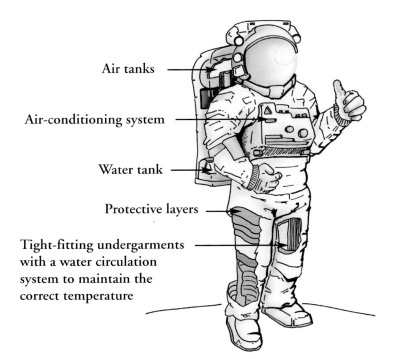

Air tanks

Air-conditioning system

Water tank

Protective layers

Tight-fitting undergarments with a water circulation system to maintain the correct temperature

Moving Around on the Moon

An astronaut loads equipment into his lunar "jeep" before setting off on a mission. He has deployed the large antenna that enables him to communicate with Earth.

The three final Apollo missions were equipped with a small vehicle called the Lunar Rover Vehicle or Lunar Jeep, which was folded away in a com-partment of the LM. When they landed and left the LM, the astronauts could unfold it and use it to travel about.

The Lunar Rover weighed 463 pounds (210 kilograms) and could transport 1,140 pounds (520 kilograms) of equipment, as well as two astronauts. It had compartments for stowing the lunar rocks they collected. It was four-wheel-drive and powered by batteries; it could climb 25-degree slopes. It was easy to drive: You pushed a lever forward to go straight ahead, to either side to turn left or right, and backward to reverse . . . just like using a computer joystick!

This vehicle enabled the astronauts to explore far from the LM. But it did not go very fast: Its top speed was 8.7 miles per hour (14 kilometers per hour). Even so, it covered a total of 53 miles (85 kilometers) during its three missions. Because the force of gravity is so weak on the Moon, the Rover might have easily gone out of control at higher speeds. Just once, the astronauts were allowed to go faster. This experiment was referred to as the "Lunar Grand Prix": the Rover traveled at over 10.5 miles per hour (17 kilometers per hour), a record which stands to this day.

The Lunar Rover Vehicle

Venus: A Living Hell

On the left, the landscape of Venus is artificially enhanced using color: The volcanoes and the lava flowing from them are a lighter shade than the plains. On the right, a close-up of the spot where a probe landed—the surface consists of volcanic lava.

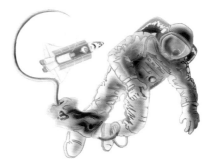

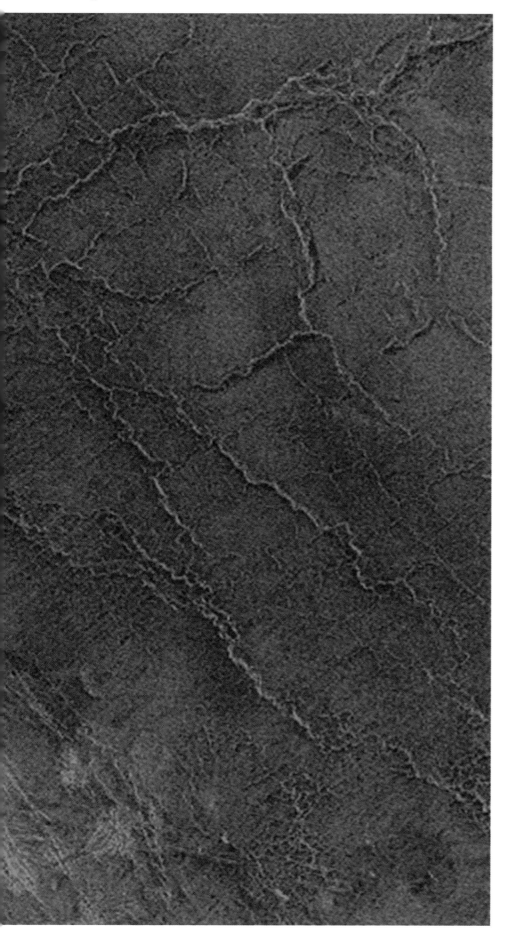

Venus is closer to the Sun than the Earth is. Its atmosphere is unbreathable, consisting of carbon dioxide with droplets of sulphuric acid floating in it at higher altitudes. It is also very hot and dense. The planet's surface is always hidden by thick cloud. The atmospheric pressure is 90 times greater than on Earth, and the temperature is 900°F (480°C)—hot enough to melt lead.

The Russians built some very robust probes to land on Venus: the *Venera* series. They had internal cooling systems so that once they landed they would last as long as possible in the intolerable conditions outside. Landing them was also a tricky problem. There was no question of using parachutes (the normal method with probes) to slow the probes' descent until they settled softly on the surface. Because Venus's atmosphere is so dense, parachutes would have slowed the probes down too much and, in the great heat, they would have broken down by the time they reached the surface. So a probe was created that, at an altitude of 30 miles (50 kilometers), would break free of its parachutes and descend on its own, with a wide band of metal attached to the top acting as a brake.

After many setbacks, ten probes were landed successfully. One even survived for over two hours on the surface. The pictures it sent back showed a landscape completely covered in gray volcanic rocks, under a yellow sky.

The *Venera* probe touches down on Venus.

Mars : A Difficult Place to Land

From the summit of a hill, the *Spirit* rover looks over the surrounding plains. In the distance are more hills and, 50 miles (80 kilometers) away and almost invisible, the rim of the vast crater in which the probe landed.

Mars is nearer to the Earth than to the Sun, but is only half as big. Its gravity is too weak to retain the kind of thick atmosphere that surrounds Earth, so the air at the surface is not very dense. It offers little resistance to parachutes, which are therefore not very effective in slowing the fall of a probe. If a traditional parachute braking system were used, the probe would come down too quickly, and smash on the planet's surface. Specially designed to land on Mars, the *Viking* probes discard their parachutes at an altitude of 4,900 feet (1,500 meters) and land with the help of small rocket engines, which slow their descent.

The *Pathfinder*, *Spirit*, and *Opportunity* probes sent to Mars use a different method to land softly on the surface: Their parachutes remain open until the last moment, then, at an altitude of 330 feet (100 meters), airbags are inflated around the probe and an enormous solid-propellant rocket fires up to slow its descent. The probe stops in mid-air and, once the rope tether (or "bridle") attaching it to the parachute is cut, drops down and bounces onto the surface, cushioned by its airbags. Once it has landed, the airbags are automatically punctured and the probe can be deployed.

The *Viking* and *Pathfinder* probes were designed to stay in one place. *Viking* had a long mechanical arm for picking up sand and testing for life on Mars. Other probes have been built to move around on the planet's surface. The small *Sojourner* rover was sent long distances by *Pathfinder* to "sniff out" interesting stones. The large rovers that accompanied the *Spirit* and *Opportunity* probes each traveled more than three miles (five kilometers), sending back amazing pictures of rocks that had once been under water. Future probes will no doubt travel hundreds of miles . . . but will they discover traces of life?

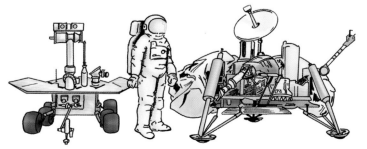

Mars Exploration Rover   *Viking* lander (1976)
(MER) (2004)

Mars: Meticulously Mapped

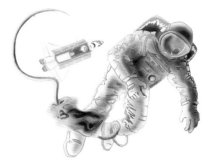

The Mars Global Surveyor probe, in orbit around Mars, flies over the giant Olympus Mons volcano, which is 370 miles (600 kilometers) across and 70,000 feet (21,000 meters) high.

The geography of Mars is spectacular, and unique in our solar system. It has similarities with both the Moon (wind-eroded craters) and the Earth (plains and volcanoes). These volcanoes are massive (up to 13 miles—21 kilometers—high), and there is one canyon cutting across a volcanic plateau which is 3,100 miles (5,000 kilometers) long and 5 miles (8 kilometers) deep. This explains why it is the most closely observed planet after the Earth. No fewer than four active probes are orbiting around it.

We also know that a great deal of water once flowed on Mars, in its early days as a planet, because our probes have discovered the beds of dried-up rivers. Mars once had a great ocean around its north pole, which froze solid when the planet's climate cooled down.

To map Mars, these probes are equipped with cameras as powerful as those used by military satellites, capable of taking sharp pictures of objects less than three feet (one meter) across. To investigate the planet's history, they also have instruments that can detect ice and define the composition of sediments deposited by water and rocks. Using laser technology, scientists have been able to produce a relief map of Mars which is as accurate as similar maps of the Earth.

Large volumes of water once flowed on Mars, as can be seen from these dried-up river beds.

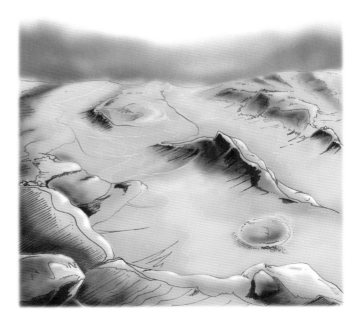

Asteroids: Flying Mountains

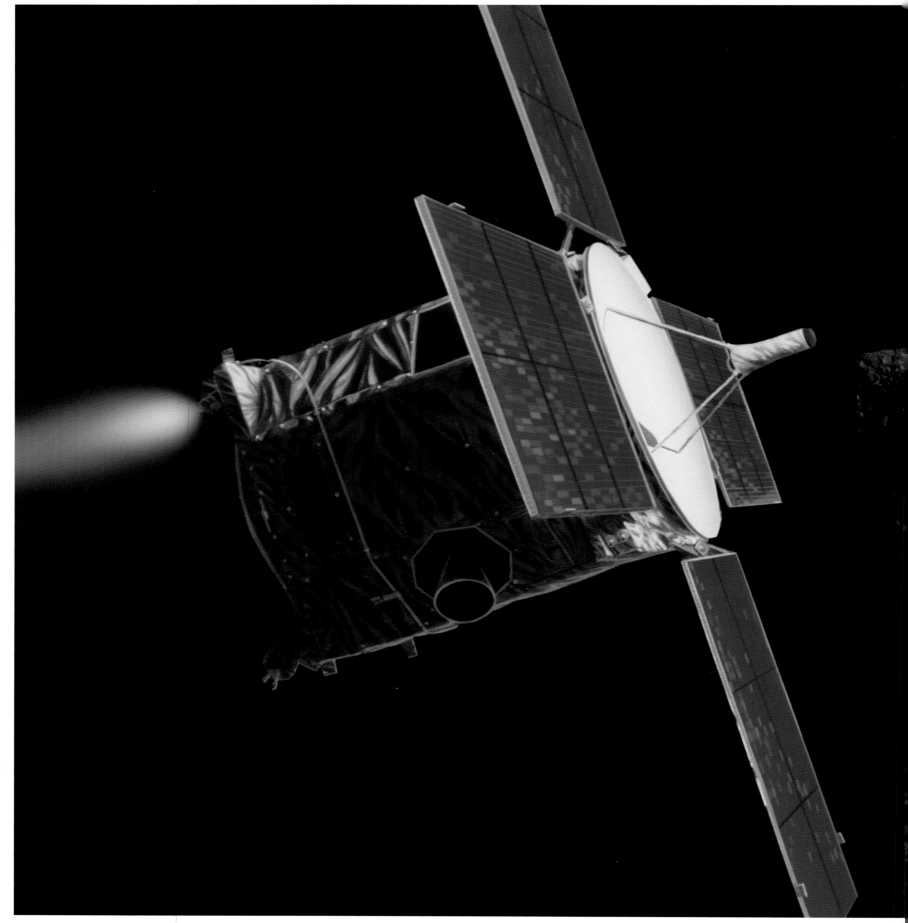

The Near Asteroid Rendezvous (NEAR) probe fires its engine to slow down and approach the asteroid Eros. This asteroid is 20 miles (33 kilometers) long, and 8 miles (13 kilometers) both wide and high—a real "flying mountain"!

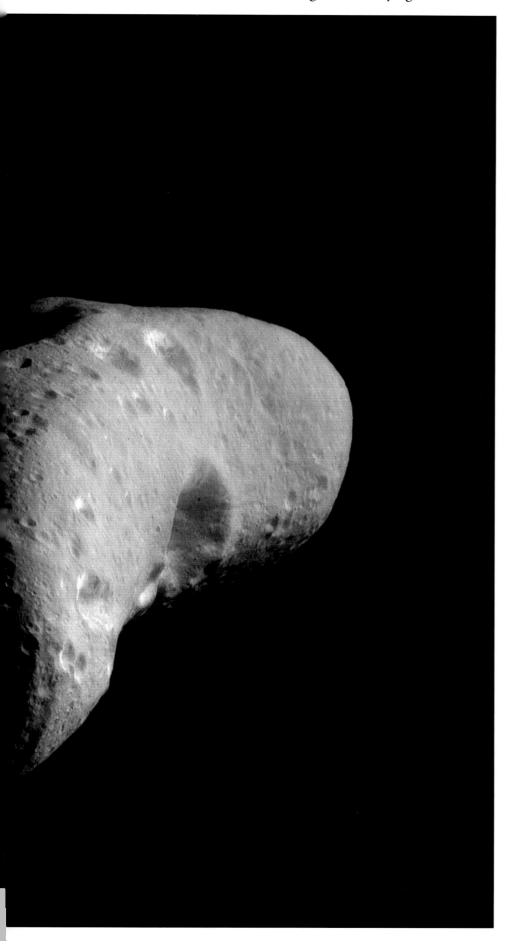

Asteroids are tiny planets, varying in size from tens to hundreds of miles across. Many of them are very irregular in shape. Almost all the asteroids in our solar system are found between the planets Mars and Jupiter. Most of them contain large amounts of metal, particularly nickel and iron. Some engineers have considered using asteroids as a source of iron; metals could easily be mined from them and transported to the Moon for building large spaceships. This would be a lot cheaper than bringing all the metal needed from Earth.

The only problem is the extremely weak gravity of these tiny planets: Explorers would have to be attached to them by cables to prevent themselves from floating away. It would be very difficult to stand upright on an asteroid, as humans would be virtually weightless. The force of gravity on an asteroid 20 miles (30 kilometers) in diameter is 1/1,200th of the gravity on Earth, so a 176-pound (80-kilogram) person would weigh just 2.5 ounces (66 grams)! A sudden movement and you would fly off into space!

Some larger asteroids also have some kind of rock, just a few miles across, orbiting around them. In other words, a mini moon for a mini planet!

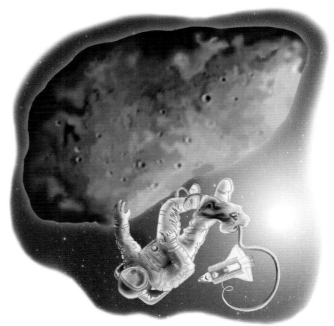

Attached by a rope to his spacecraft, this astronaut is taking a sample of material from an asteroid.

Penetrating Jupiter

The *Galileo* probe passes close to Io, Jupiter's large volcanic satellite. It has just launched a smaller probe, which creates a shooting star as it penetrates the atmosphere of the giant planet.

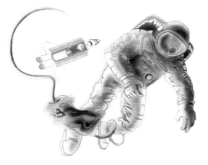

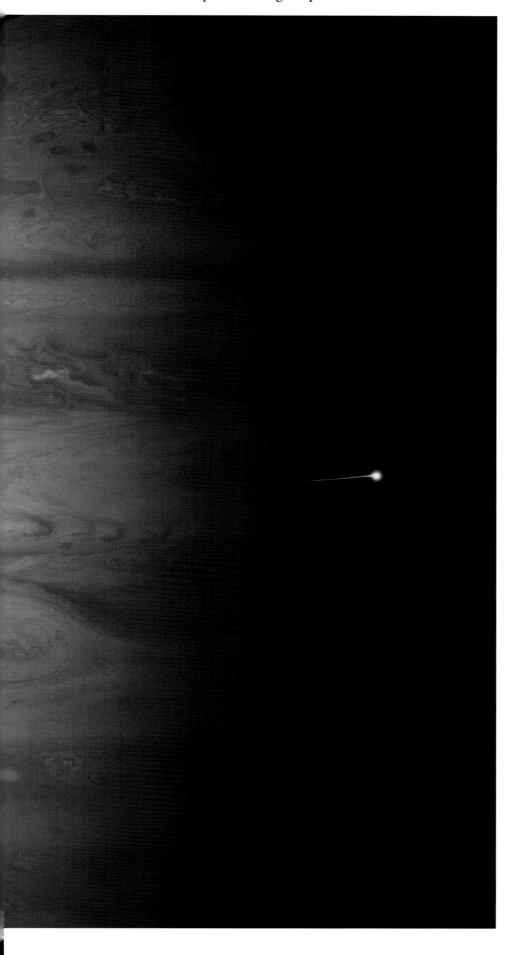

Jupiter is a giant of a planet, eleven times the size of the Earth, but composed solely of gases. It does not have a solid surface like Venus, Earth, or Mars. There is no ground to stand on. Rather than land on Jupiter, you would sink into its progressively thicker atmosphere (consisting of hydrogen and helium), coming under increasing pressure and experiencing higher and higher temperatures.

Jupiter is a very special planet. At its center, it is almost as hot as the Sun, and yet it does not have the Sun's brightness. Scientists describe Jupiter as a "failed" sun, because it is not large enough to trigger the nuclear reactions that take place at the heart of our Sun.

To explore this strange planet it was therefore necessary to build an extremely tough and resistant probe. It arrived from Earth at a speed of 105,000 miles per hour (170,000 kilometers per hour) and, as it braked violently on meeting Jupiter's atmosphere, its protective shield had to withstand temperatures of 25,200°F (14,000°C). Two minutes later, it was traveling at only 615 miles per hour (990 kilometers per hour). A parachute then opened to slow it down further, and its scientific instruments began to take readings. An hour later, having been tossed around by 310-mile-per-hour (500-kilometer-per-hour) winds, the probe was 93 miles (150 kilometers) into Jupiter's atmosphere. At this altitude, the temperature was already 307°F (153°C) and the atmospheric pressure 22 times that on Earth. Under this extreme pressure, the probe eventually broke down.

The *Galileo* probe penetrates Jupiter's atmosphere.

Titan: Fog, Wind, and Ice

The European *Huygens* probe, attached to its parachute, descends onto Titan, Saturn's large satellite. Here it is 15 miles (25 kilometers) above the surface, with ancient rivers of methane down below.

Landing on Titan, Saturn's largest moon, which is .93 billion miles (1.5 billion kilometers) from Earth, once seemed an impossible feat. But after a dramatic descent lasting two hours and 28 minutes, the European space probe *Huygens* eventually got there. Things went badly from the beginning: Ten minutes after entering Titan's foggy atmosphere, the probe, which was designed to spin like a top to keep it stable, started spinning in the wrong direction. The problem was caused by the breaking of one of its parachute cables. Consequently, *Huygens* was tossed in all directions by violent turbulence, with winds blowing at more than 230 miles per hour (400 kilometers per hour) Contrary to expectations, the camera showed only clouds, rather than Titan's surface. Suddenly, at an altitude of around 18 miles (30 kilometers), *Huygens* emerged from the fog. But then there was another problem: 3.7 miles (6 kilometers) from the surface, the probe, driven by an opposing wind, changed direction. Would the parachute get tangled up? Fortunately not.

The probe finally touched down at a speed of 8.7 miles per hour (14 kilometers per hour), landing in frozen mud. All in all, its small camera sent back 606 pictures, 230 of them after the probe had landed. It managed to survive for a few hours on Titan's surface in icy cold temperatures of minus 290°F (minus 179°C). Around it lay blocks of dirty ice, recently deposited there by torrents containing a liquid mixture of water, ammonia, and methane. In such cold temperatures and under pressures one-and-a-half times those on Earth, strange chemical reactions take place. On Titan, methane, present on Earth as a gas, is a liquid, while water is transformed into ice harder than rock.

The *Huygens* probe reaches Titan. Exploration can begin at last!

Uranus: Near the Rings

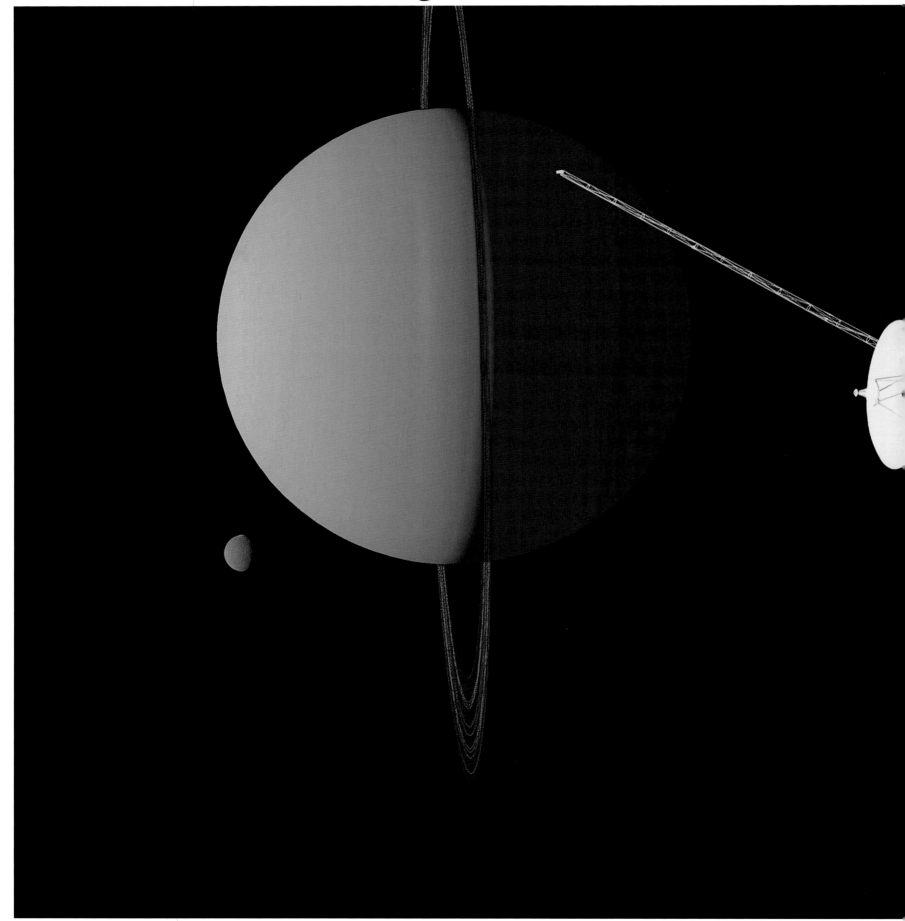

The *Voyager 2* probe flies over Miranda, one of the satellites of Uranus. In the background, you can see the planet and its rings, as well as Umbriel, another of its five satellites.

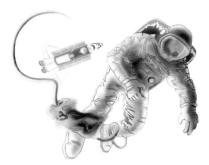

Four times the size of Earth, the gaseous planet Uranus is quite unique. It spins with one pole turned toward the Sun and the other plunged in darkness. The same is true of its delicate rings and moons. Uranus orbits the Sun once every 168 years. Its north and south poles therefore alternate in facing the Sun, taking turns every 84 years.

After the space probe *Voyager 2* flew past Saturn, NASA decided to send it to Uranus, knowing that it would be able to observe only its southern hemisphere, which was lit by the Sun at the time. The probe eventually faced Uranus's south pole; it was almost dark at the planet's equator. The same was true of Uranus's moons, but, as they turn around its equator, some were above and some below Uranus, rather than being behind or in front, as they would have been in the case of a normal planet. The probe's camera therefore had to be much more angled than normal in order to observe them. And the pictures had to be taken in a very short space of time, since the probe was traveling at more than 31,000 miles per hour (50,000 kilometers per hour).

And that was not the only problem: Uranus is so far from the Sun that there is very little light, even at the pole directly facing it (the planet receives 1/370th of the amount of light reaching Earth). *Voyager 2's* computer had to be reprogrammed to enable its camera to "see" the planet and all its moons. The operation was a great success, with Voyager sending back the first pictures of Miranda, the roughest moon in the whole solar system. Miranda is not even round, and has gigantic cliffs more than 9.3 miles (15 kilometers) high cutting across it.

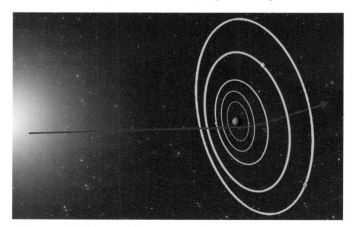

The path followed by *Voyager 2* takes it close to the rings of Uranus.

Neptune: A Cold, Dark Giant

The *Voyager 2* probe has just flown over Triton, Neptune's enormous satellite. In the background, you can see the gaint, icy planet with its rings.

Neptune is both giant and very distant from the Earth. It is the same size as Uranus, but its atmosphere is a great deal more active, with winds blowing at over 1,240 miles per hour (2,000 kilometers per hour)! The *Voyager 2* mission was again faced with a tremendous challenge, working in extremely difficult conditions where the sun's light is 900 times weaker than on Earth. Neptune also has five very fine rings around its equator, consisting of small blocks of ice. *Voyager 2* had to dodge them, or it would have been smashed to smithereens. The probe managed to avoid the rings and scraped past the north pole of the planet at a distance of no more than 2,480 miles (4,000 kilometers).

Voyager 2 then traveled past Neptune's moon Triton, at a distance of 24,800 miles (40,000 kilometers). This large satellite was still a mystery, and scientists were counting on *Voyager* to tell them more about it. They discovered that it is only 1,680 miles (2,710 kilometers) across—so smaller than our own Moon, which has a diameter of 2,180 miles (3,500 kilometers). The temperature there is so cold—minus 390°F (minus 235°C)—that the surface is covered in an icy mixture of frozen water and methane. Enormous geysers of liquid nitrogen create huge dark streaks, blown by the feeble winds of Triton's very thin atmosphere. Scientists now think that Triton was a planet in its own right, similar to Pluto, but was "captured" by Neptune during the early history of our solar system.

Before the probe passed close to Triton, engineers worked out the best strategy for observing it. Each square corresponds to a photograph to be taken by the probe.

Pluto: Surviving Away from the Sun

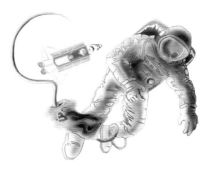

This computer-generated image shows the *New Horizons* probe flying over Pluto and its large satellite Charon, an event planned for 2015.

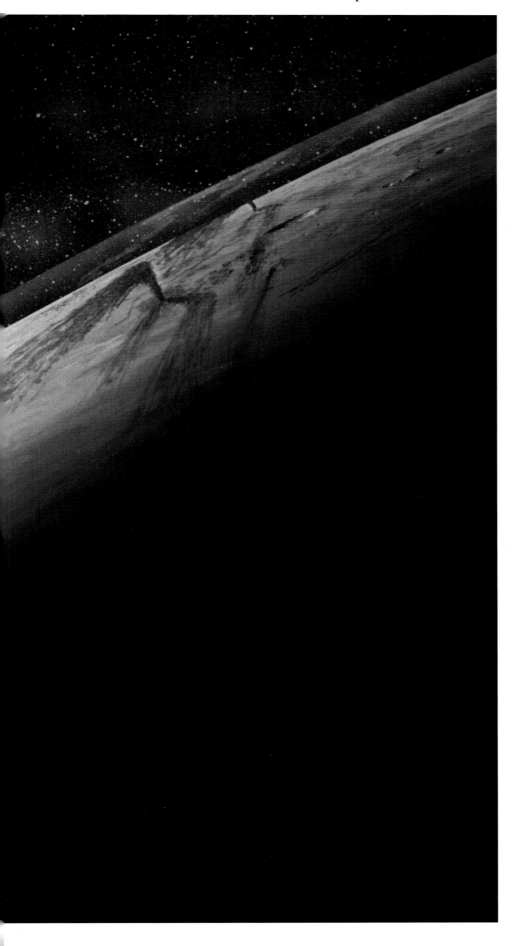

As it orbits the Sun, Pluto is between 2.73 and 4.53 billion miles (4.4 and 7.3 billion kilometers) from the Earth. The distance is so enormous that it would take several decades for a normal probe to reach it. Since an ordinary probe would not survive the long journey, scientists have built an extremely solid probe to travel to Pluto, called *New Horizons*. As well as surviving the long journey, the probe has to be able to withstand the terrible cold that prevails in the most remote and dark parts of our solar system. To prevent its freezing in transit, it has been insulated rather like a thermos flask. For greater speed, it is also very lightweight.

It will fly past Pluto at 26,700 miles per hour (43,000 kilometers per hour), just ten years after leaving the Earth. Near Pluto light from the Sun is so weak (1,100 times weaker than on Earth), that solar panels couldn't generate the electricity needed by the probe. Instead, it has a small nuclear power unit.

Launched in February 2006, *New Horizons* will fly past Pluto on July 14, 2015, at a distance of 6,000 miles (9,600 kilometers), then past Charon, Pluto's biggest moon, at a distance of 16,700 miles (27,000 kilometers). Strangely, Pluto (1,500 miles—2,400 kilometers—in diameter) and Charon (745 miles—1,200 kilometers—in diameter) are so close that they circle each other in just a few days. This mission should therefore produce plenty of surprises, including the first ever pictures of Pluto's thin atmosphere, which is composed of nitrogen.

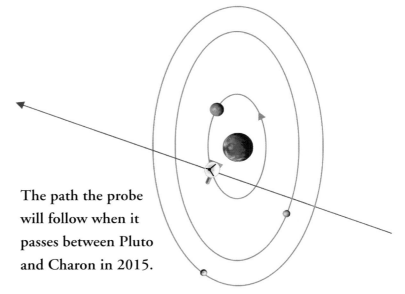

The path the probe will follow when it passes between Pluto and Charon in 2015.

Living on the Moon

These astronauts have driven to the top of a hill in their "jeep" to observe progress in the construction of their new lunar base. A rocket can be seen about to land and deliver another module, making the base a more comfortable place in which to live and work.

Before sending humans to Mars, in a hypothetical future, scientists plan to test the endurance and technical capacities of the spacecraft involved on the Moon. To get to the Moon, astronauts will start their journey from a space station orbiting the Earth. This makes the journey to the Moon easier and less expensive. Maybe one day a base will be built on the Moon, in a spot where there is water. Water can in fact be found on the Moon, deposited by comets which have crashed there in the past (comets are made of ice). This ice has been preserved in the vicinity of the poles, where the sun never shines into the Moon's craters. Elsewhere, the Moon is totally dry.

For their own needs, and to fuel the rocket engines of their spacecraft, the astronauts will produce oxygen by collecting soil from the Moon's surface and crushing it into fine powder: 40 percent of it is oxygen. It will be possible to extract and bottle this oxygen, then send it to the space station orbiting the Earth to fuel the spacecraft that will later travel to Mars. The most efficient rocket engines consume 13 pounds (six kilograms) of oxygen for every pound (half a kilogram) of hydrogen. Bringing oxygen from the Moon is more economical than transporting it from Earth, because everything weighs less on the Moon (one sixth of its weight on Earth), therefore less energy is required to transport it.

2017: another "space train" taking six astronauts to the Moon!

A City in Space

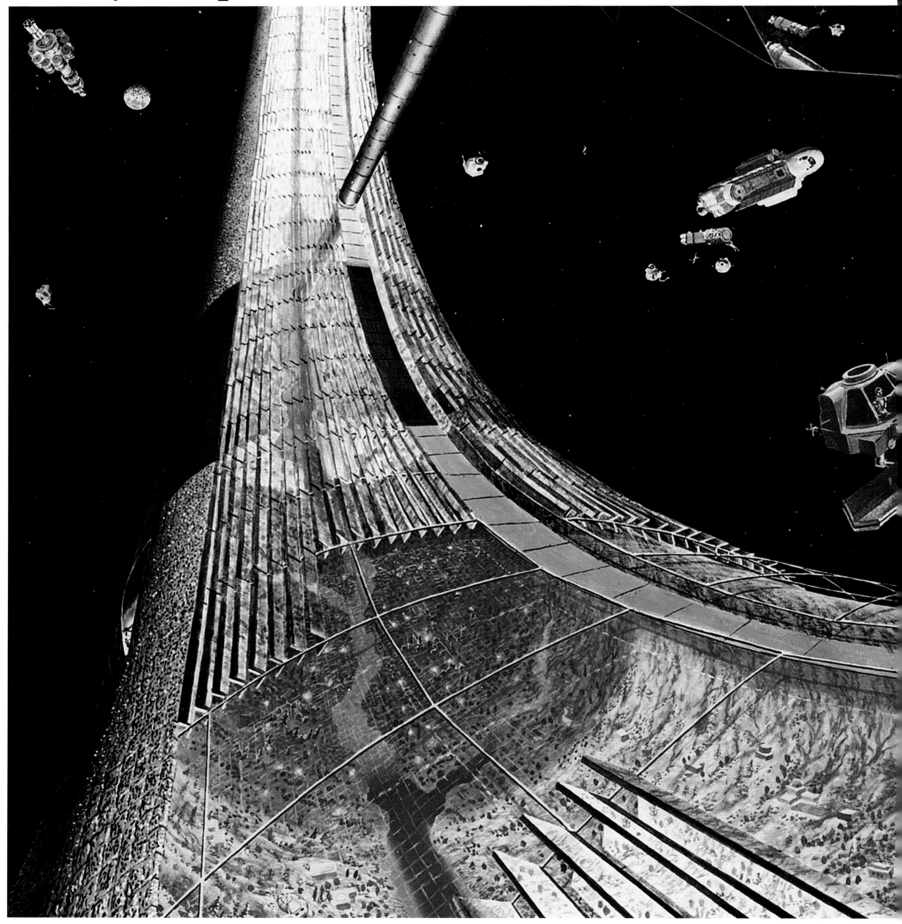

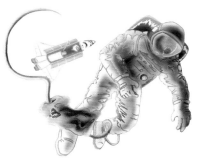

This wheel-shaped structure houses a city orbiting the Earth. It is so big that we can see only a small part of it, with its rivers and fields.

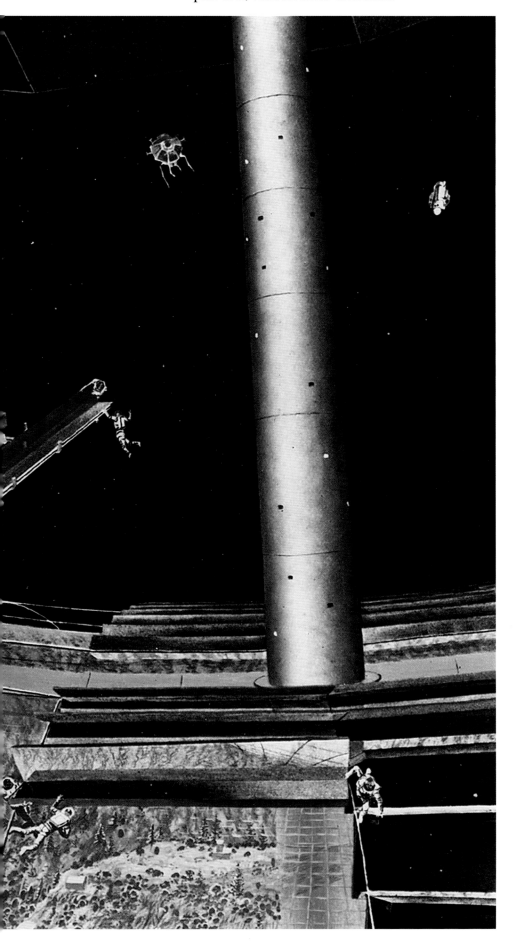

Thirty-five years ago, the visionary Gerard O'Neill suggested a new way of colonizing space—by building several huge cities. To keep them orbiting the Earth without crashing into it or drifting away, they would have to be built in places where the Earth's and Moon's forces of gravity cancel each other out.

Each city would be wheel-shaped. If the cities were made to turn on their own axes, at a speed of one rotation every five minutes, an artificial gravity would be created, ensuring that people and objects had weight and did not float. It would therefore be possible to stand up and move around normally. The inside of the wheel would be hollow and lined with houses. There would be rivers, and people would grow crops, just as on Earth! The inhabitants would soon forget they were living inside a giant wheel in space.

On the outside of the wheel, mirrors hung like curtains would follow the sun and reflect its light inward. Every evening, they would be turned in the other direction to create an artificial "night" for the colonists. In the morning, they would be angled toward the Sun once again. A colony of this kind could support a million people, who would be able to live in great comfort and with a considerable degree of independence (only a minimum of resources would need to be brought from Earth) . . . provided they looked after their city's environment and were careful not to pollute it.

The First People on Mars

1. Landing modules on Mars; 2. setting up the first base; 3. taking off from Mars; and 4. docking with a spaceship for the return journey to Earth. All adventures awaiting the first Martian astronauts!

How will we send people to Mars? The mission is dangerous, but NASA has approved the following operation: automated, unmanned cargo ships will first set out for Mars on reconnaissance flights, accompanied by spaceships, unmanned for now but intended to bring the astronauts back at a later stage. They will take ten months to reach Mars. Then the astronauts will join them, traveling in a habitable module and taking a quicker route (seven months).

When they arrive on Mars, the astronauts will find their return spacecraft, which is equipped with a nuclear reactor, already producing electricity. It will have been programmed to start up a small unit which processes the carbon dioxide in the Martian atmosphere (the atmosphere is 95 percent carbon dioxide) and extracts from it the oxygen needed by the engines of their spacecraft when its blasts off on the return journey. A large, wheeled, pressurized vehicle will also have been sent in advance, so the astronauts will be able to start exploring as soon as they arrive. These and the habitable module in which they land on Mars make up all the elements of a mini base for the astronauts.

A month later, other automated spaceships will land near them, bringing equipment and additional modules in case of any breakdowns. The smallest technical hitch could put the astronauts in danger, and the Earth would be too far away to provide help.

The astronauts will work in a laboratory module, analyzing rocks and trying to discover if there is life on Mars. The real adventure begins when they get there.

Building a Base on Mars

An astronaut examines a stone in the hope of finding fossils. In the background, you can see the modules of the base in which the crew lives, and the vehicles in which they get around and explore.

Modules will be assembled on Mars to form the "nucleus" of a base. They will be covered with Martian soil to protect them from harmful solar radiation, since Mars does not have the thick ozone layer and magnetic field that protect us from radiation here on Earth. Finally, systems will be installed to recycle air, water, and waste products. The power will be supplied by a small nuclear power station. The colonists will have settled in a spot where it is possible to extract ice or water from underground.

Some modules will not be made of metal, but will be inflatable structures pumped up with Martian air. They will be made of a special plastic which hardens by itself in time—a good way of avoiding punctures! Some of these modules will serve as greenhouses for growing plants, because the menu on Mars will be a vegetarian one. Crops will be cultivated in large tanks. It will even be possible to raise fish to add some protein to the diet. The colonists will have become true "Martians."

How a base on Mars might look.

Traveling to Another Star

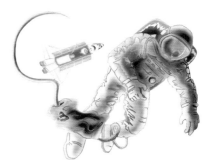

An explorer spaceship enters the atmosphere of a new planet akin to Earth. The landscape inspires mixed feelings of strangeness and familiarity.

Since the 1950s, engineers have been dreaming of interstellar travel, voyaging to other stars like our Sun to discover the mysterious planets that circle them. They hope to find living beings, or even other civilizations. Such travel is far from simple, as the distances involved are enormous. The nearest star to us, Alpha Centauri, is 4.3 light years away (meaning its light takes 4.3 years to reach us), 270,000 times the distance separating the Earth from the Sun!

To undertake a journey of this kind, a spaceship would have to be launched at the speed of light: 186,282 miles per second (299,792 kilometers per second)—an impossibility. Otherwise, the journey would take too long and the crew would die on the way. Our present technology is inadequate: The fastest spacecraft can travel at 67 million miles per hour (108 million kilometers per hour), barely 10 percent of light speed. Traveling at top speed, it would take today's spaceships 43 years to reach Alpha Centauri. In other words, the crew would never come back to Earth alive—unless we sent babies. The astronauts would have to live tightly packed together in their spacecraft, and would not be able to get out until they arrived. This would undoubtedly give rise to food shortages, serious quarrels, maybe even mutiny.

The only way to avoid these dangers would be to put the astronauts to sleep artificially for the duration of the journey, or cause them to "hibernate" to slow down the aging process. But these techniques (high-speed propulsion, hibernation, deep-freezing astronauts!) have not yet been developed.

It will probably be several centuries before so great an adventure can be undertaken.

To my wife Edith and my children Maÿlis, Caroline, Christian, Henry and Philippe. You have all joined me in my adventures in space and this is the book I would have liked to have given you a long time ago… Many thanks to Éditions Tallendier for helping me to get started on this project. —O.G